P9-CEV-992

For Elisabeth Marie, may you always have a sense of wonder!
- M. B. -

To the children, teachers, parents and staff at the Columbus School for Girls - Thank you for ten
inspiring years filled with joy, creativity and endless possibilities!
- J. C. -

The author wishes to thank the Florida Oceanographic Coastal Center (www.floridaoceanographic.org)
for their help in reviewing the manuscript for this book.

Copyright © 2004 Marianne Berkes · Illustrations © 2004 Jeanette Canyon · All rights reserved.
Dawn Publications · 12402 Bitney Springs Road · Nevada City, CA 95959 · nature@dawnpub.com

Library of Congress Cataloging-in-Publication Data
Berkes, Marianne Collins.
Over in the ocean : in a coral reef / by Marianne Berkes ; illustrated by Jeanette Canyon. --1st ed.
p. cm.
Based on the traditional song "Over in the meadow."
ISBN 1-58469-062-3 (pbk.) --- ISBN 1-58469-063-1 (hardcover)
I. Canyon, Jeanette, 1965 - ill. II. Title.
PZ7.B45570v 2004   2004003650

Book Design & Production by Jeanette & Christopher Canyon
Original Art Photographed by Jeff Rose

First Edition
10 9 8 7

Manufactured by Regent Publishing Services, Hong Kong
Printed July 2010 in ShenZhen, Guangdong, China

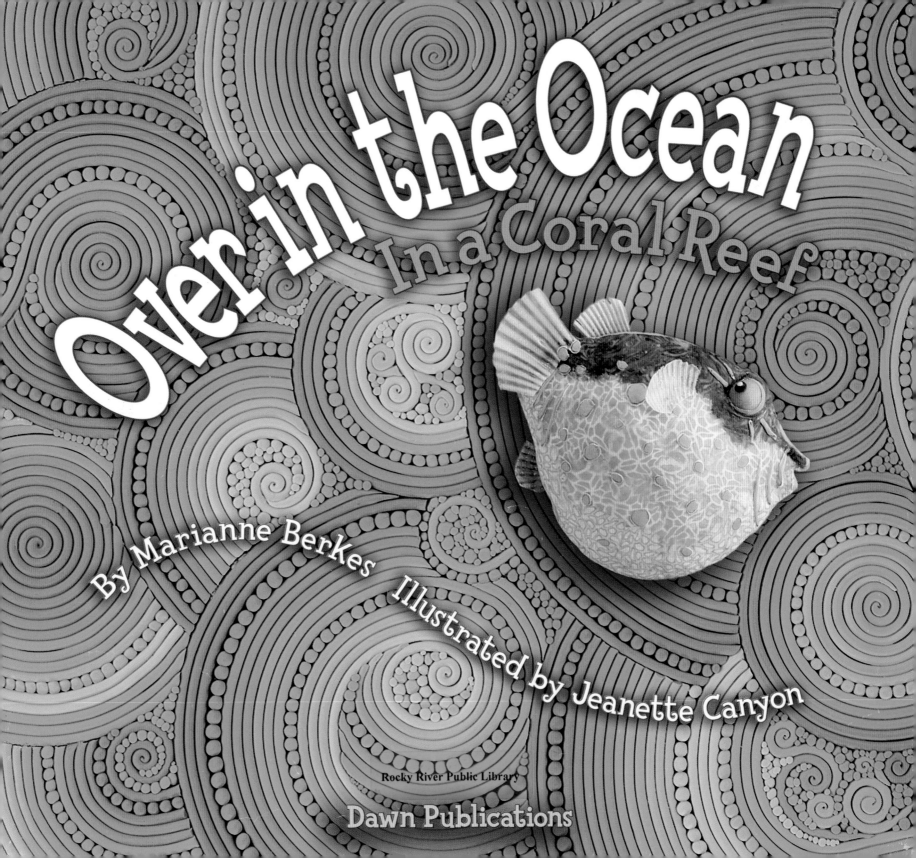

Over in the Ocean
In a Coral Reef

By Marianne Berkes   Illustrated by Jeanette Canyon

Rocky River Public Library

Dawn Publications

Over in the ocean
Far away from the sun
Lived a mother octopus
And her octopus one.

"Squirt," said the mother.
"I squirt," said the one.
So they squirted in the reef
Far away from the sun.

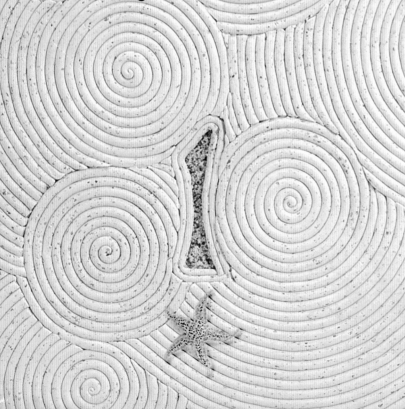

Over in the ocean
Where the sea grasses grew
Lived a mother parrotfish
And her parrotfish two.

"Grind," said the mother.
"We grind," said the two.
So they ground on the coral
Where the sea grasses grew.

Over in the ocean
In a sea anemone
Lived an old mother clownfish
And her little clownfish three.

"Dart," said the mother.
"We dart," said the three.
So they darted all around
In a sea anemone.

Over in the ocean
On a sandy sea floor
Lived an old mother stingray
And her little stingrays four.

"Stir," said the mother.
"We stir," said the four.
So they stirred with their fins
On a sandy sea floor.

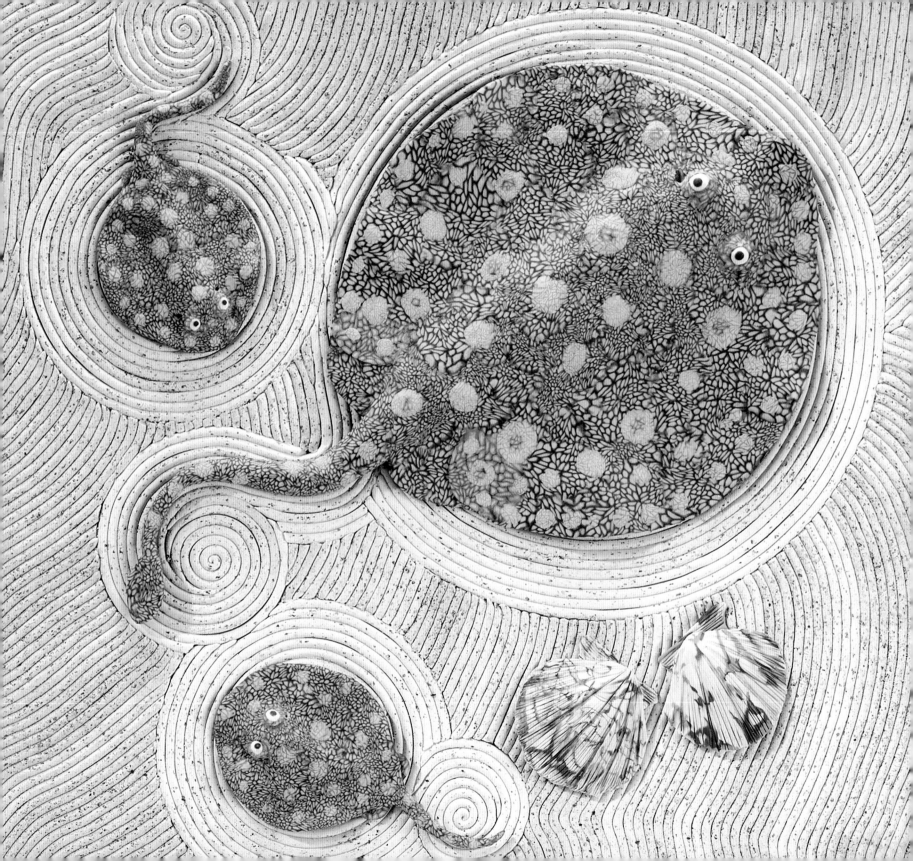

Over in the ocean
Where the scuba divers dive
Lived an old mother puffer
And her pufferfish five.

"Puff," said the mother.
"We puff," said the five.
So they puffed in and out
Where the scuba divers dive.

Over in the ocean
Doing somersault tricks
Lived an old mother dolphin
And her little dolphins six.

"Jump," said the mother.
"We jump," said the six.
So they jumped and they played
Doing somersault tricks.

6

Over in the ocean
In their sea fan heaven
Lived a mother angelfish
And her little angels seven.

"Graze," said the mother.
"We graze," said the seven.
So they lazed and they grazed
In their sea fan heaven.

Over in the ocean
Very streamlined and straight
Lived a mother needlefish
And her needlefish eight.

"Skitter," said the mother.
"We skitter," said the eight.
So they skittered through the water
Very streamlined and straight.

Over in the ocean
Drifting in a yellow line
Lived an old mother gruntfish
And her little grunts nine.

"Grunt," said the mother.
"We grunt," said the nine.
So they grunted and they kissed
Drifting in a yellow line.

Over in the ocean
In their turtle grass den
Lived an old father seahorse
And his seahorses ten.

"Flutter," said the father.
"We flutter," said the ten.
So they fluttered all around
In their turtle grass den.

Over in the ocean
Where the sea creatures play
While their parents all were resting
They up and swam away!

"Find us," said the children,
"From ten to one!"
When you find all the creatures
Then this rhyme is done.

10
9
8
7
6
5
4
3
2
1

Over in the Ocean

sung to the tune
"Over in the Meadow"

Traditional tune
words by Marianne Berkes

O-ver in the o-cean far a-way from the sun, Lived a mother oc-to-pus and her oc-to-pus one,

"Squirt," said the mother. "I squirt," said the one. So they squirted in the reef, far a-way from the sun.

2. Over in the ocean where the sea grasses grew
Lived a mother *parrotfish* and her parrotfish two.
"Grind," said the mother.
"We grind," said the two.
So they ground on the coral where the sea grasses grew.

3. Over in the ocean in a sea anemone
Lived an old mother *clownfish* and her little clownfish three.
"Dart," said the mother.
"We dart," said the three.
So they darted all around in a sea anemone.

4. Over in the ocean on a sandy sea floor
Lived an old mother *stingray* and her little stingrays four.
"Stir," said the mother.
"We stir," said the four.
So they stirred with their fins on a sandy sea floor.

5. Over in the ocean where the scuba divers dive
Lived an old mother *puffer* and her puffer fish five.
"Puff," said the mother.
"We puff," said the five.
So they puffed in and out where the scuba divers dive.

6. Over in the ocean doing somersault tricks
Lived an old mother *dolphin* and her little dolphins six.
"Jump," said the mother.
"We jump," said the six.
So they jumped and they played doing somersault tricks.

7. Over in the ocean in their sea fan heaven
Lived a mother *angelfish* and her little angels seven.
"Graze," said the mother.
"We graze," said the seven.
So they lazed and they grazed in their sea fan heaven.

8. Over in the ocean very streamlined and straight
Lived a mother *needlefish* and her needlefish eight.
"Skitter," said the mother.
"We skitter," said the eight.
So they skittered through the water very streamlined and straight.

9. Over in the ocean drifting in a yellow line
Lived an old mother *gruntfish* and her little grunts nine.
"Grunt," said the mother.
"We grunt," said the nine.
So they grunted and they kissed drifting in a yellow line.

10. Over in the ocean in their turtle grass den
Lived an old father *seahorse* and his seahorses ten.
"Flutter," said the father.
"We flutter," said the ten.
So they fluttered all around in their turtle grass den.

11. Over in the ocean where the sea creatures play
While their parents all were resting they up and swam away.
"Find us," said the children,
"From ten to one!"
When you find all the creatures then this rhyme is done.

How Many Babies Do They *Really* Have?

Usually, quite a few! The rhyme in this book is based on the popular 19th century song "Over in the Meadow" by Olive A. Wadsworth. In this coral reef adaptation of the song, the animals really do squirt, grind, dart, etc., as they have been portrayed—but the number of babies they have is very different.

A few sea creatures (such as dolphins) are mammals, and have one or two babies at a time and care for them diligently. Most sea creatures, however, reproduce by laying eggs—sometimes thousands, or hundreds of thousands, at a time. For example, the octopus vulgaris, found off the west coast of Florida, lays over 200,000 eggs in long strings that are attached to reef rocks, which she guards until they hatch. Then she dies and the babies are on their own. The eggs of the seahorse are treated very specially! Read more about them in the section that begins on the next page.

Generally, the more babies there are, the less parental help is available, so that among sea creatures, only some parents guard their eggs or take care of their young. Many others leave them completely alone, in which case only a few survive to grow up. Nature has very different ways of ensuring the survival of different species.

The Coral Reef Community

Did you know that a tiny creature—the coral polyp—is responsible for the existence of the entire coral reef community? Even though coral polyps look like plants, they are tiny animals that attach themselves to a hard surface and immediately begin producing limestone to protect their bodies. Other polyps grow and eventually become a coral colony, an underwater garden that provides a habitat for the greatest diversity of species in the ocean. In this way, coral reefs are like the tropical rainforests of the sea. But it takes thousands of years for these coral colonies to form. Unfortunately people are destroying many of these special places. To learn about 25 things you can do to protect coral reefs, please go online to www.publicaffairs.noaa.gov/25list.html.

About the Coral Reef

Octopuses have eight arms coming out from the head, around the mouth. Each arm has two rows of suckers, which gives a very strong grip. They have no bones, but they have relatively large brains and are probably the most intelligent of all animals without a backbone (invertebrates). When they feel threatened by an enemy, octopuses *squirt* dark ink from a special sac into the water, forming an "ink cloud" behind which they can escape. They can move by jet propulsion, by shooting a stream of water in one direction, which propels them the opposite way. Octopuses live in many parts of the ocean, and like to hide in crevasses in coral reefs.

Parrotfish live mostly on coral reefs in shallow water. Looking somewhat dull when young, they become more colorful as they grow older - almost as colorful as the birds after which they are named. Parrotfish also change their sex as they age. Their teeth are fused, forming a "beak" which they use to bite off pieces of coral. They then *grind* the coral thoroughly.

Clownfish live among beautiful sea anemones (pronounced a-NEM-o-nees). Sea anemones look like flowers that wave their "petals" in the moving water, but the petals are actually poisonous tentacles that stun the prey that they eat. Unlike other small reef fishes, clownfish are not harmed because they are protected by a slimy substance. The colorful clownfish spends most of its life *darting* around the sea anemones, attracting would-be predators that the anemone then eats. Clownfish live only in the Pacific Ocean.

Stingrays look like wavy flat disks with long, whiplike tails. They are graceful swimmers and look almost as if they are flying through the water. They like to *stir* the sandy ocean floor with their fins to find and feed on worms, mussels and small crustaceans that live there. When they lie flat on the sand, they can be hard to see. If you are wading in a sandy area, shuffle your feet to make the ray swim away. Stingrays have a double-serrated spiny barb on their tails, and although they use it only in self-defense, it can inflict a serious wound.

Pufferfish - As you might guess by its name, this fish can *puff* up its body by swallowing lots of water or air until it is inflated like a balloon. If it fills itself with air, it floats helplessly at the surface and cannot swim until the air is released. It is a clumsy swimmer anyway, for a fish. Puffers are common in coral reefs where they feed on sea urchins and crustaceans with their tough teeth. Some puffers are very poisonous to eat.

Animals in this Book

Dolphins are mammals that nurse their young, which are born live - unlike most fish, which are hatched from eggs. Bottlenose dolphins, as illustrated in this book, are often seen in and around coral reefs. They have pointed snouts with bulbous heads and streamlined bodies. As with all mammals, dolphins breathe air. When they come to the surface to breathe, they often playfully dive and *jump*, putting on quite a show!

Angelfish are brightly colored with flat, thin bodies. They are friendly and curious, and sometimes swim right up to people who are snorkeling. Angelfish often blend in with water plants and sea fans (a type of coral) as they *graze* about the reefs. The angelfish is often considered one of the most beautiful of all fishes. There are many types that vary greatly in color and pattern. The Emperor angelfish, perhaps so named because it looks so regal, is the one illustrated in this book. Because they are so beautiful, angelfish are often sold for display in fish tanks.

Needlefish are easily identified by their very long, thin bodies. Some kinds of needlefish grow to a length of five feet. Needlefish have beaklike jaws with relatively large sharp teeth. Most needlefish pass through a "halfbeak" stage in their development, in which the lower jaw, but not the upper jaw, is greatly extended. They swim in small schools and are most active at night. They are surface dwellers and *skitter* over the water in pursuit of smaller fishes.

Gruntfish are tropical fish with relatively large heads and yellow lines on their oblong bodies. There are around 150 species of grunts. They earned their name because of the grunting sound they make when they grind their teeth together. Grunts *drift* over reefs and rocks in small to large schools and often stay in formation. Some species *"kiss"* when they approach each other with their mouths wide open. This is thought to be a form of courtship.

Seahorses are among the oddest of all fish. Their heads and necks look somewhat like horses. After the mother seahorse lays her eggs, the father carries them in his pouch until they hatch and swim out. Seahorses swim by using the dorsal fin on their backs and pectoral fins on each side of their heads. It takes seahorses thousands of fin beats just to move a few inches. They move upright, *fluttering* their tails, which work like propellers. They depend on camouflage to hide from predators and wrap their tails around turtle grass when they are not moving.

Tips from the Author

I hope you will read "Over in the Ocean" often, each time discovering something new and exciting. A great reward as a visiting children's author and storyteller, is to hear a child shout, "Read it, again!" This book offers many opportunities for extended activities. Here are a few ideas.

In addition to counting the main sea creatures, be sure to look for other coral plants and animals to find and count. Sometimes I use an autoharp and sing the story. Puppets are great "story stretchers." Children can draw and cut out their own sea creatures and make them into stick puppets. As you read or sing the rhyme, each child can act out the story with his/her fish. At the end, all the sea creatures are raised up as they swim away, creating a coral reef.

Here is a special treat that I've written especially for this book - **Fingerplay Fun!**
As you sing or read the story, invite the children to use different finger or hand movements for each fish's action, like this:

Octopuses "squirt": Squeeze both hands as if you are squirting something.
Parrotfish "grind": Place thumbs under fingers and move back and forth in a grinding motion.
Clownfish "dart": Place hands together as if praying and move quickly back and forth.
Stingrays "stir": Make fists with both hands and stir in a circular motion.
Pufferfish "puff": Touch fingertips together to make a ball and open and close.
Dolphins "jump": Shape hands like dolphins and make them jump. At the end of this verse, roll hands as if doing a somersault.
Angelfish "graze": Put hands together again as you did with darting, but this time move very slowly.
Needlefish "skitter": Put arms way out straight. Then separate arms and wiggle fingers in a skittering motion.
Gruntfish "grunt and kiss": Place thumbs under other fingers and open and shut in a snapping motion; then point fingers together as if kissing.
Seahorses "flutter": Move fingers as if playing the piano in a fluttering motion.

Of course, best of all is to visit a coral reef, or your nearest aquarium, where you will see many of the amazing sea creatures that are in this book. My website is www.MarianneBerkes.com. I would love to hear from teachers and parents with creative ways to use this book.

Tips from the Artist

The art in this book was shaped entirely from polymer clay. As a picture book artist and former early childhood arts educator, I believe that polymer clay is a wonderful, friendly, pliable and colorful medium for both children and adults to work with. As a fine artist, I love to create art with an array of colors, patterns and textures, and to make things with my hands - just as children do!

My studio is actually a lot like a kitchen. In a refrigerator I store the clay. I should say "polymer clay" because it is not like clay dug from the earth, but it is actually a clay-like material. I have a variety of shaping tools including a pasta machine, food processors, cake decorating tools and other utensils. And there is even an oven in which the clay is baked after the pictures are pieced together. The original art for the pictures in this book are not flat, which is very satisfying to me because it speaks to my love of both sculpting and painting. The art is called a "relief:" sculpted pieces projecting from a flat surface. To create the two-dimensional illustrations for a book, the reliefs are photographed (with careful attention to lighting).

Polymer clay offers children a unique way to communicate their ideas, as well as to experiment with and learn about color mixing. You will find many colors available in art and hobby stores – even some translucent and glow-in-the-dark colors. I suggest that you "play" with a few shaping tools and color mixes yourself – and the children will be right there with their own creative approaches. I like to visit schools and would love to see some of your own creations. Contact me through the "Authors & Illustrators" section of Dawn Publications' website, www.dawnpub.com.

Find the clownfish towards the beginning of this book. Can you see the tiny fish scales on their bodies? I created this texture by pressing a plastic mesh bag that once held cherry tomatoes into the clay.

Look closely at the seahorse on the front cover. Can you see that it is made of little pieces with patterns that look like a kaleidoscope? They are made of "canes" mixed and rolled from different colors of clay, then sliced into thin pieces.

Sometimes I add things to the clay for special effects. Look closely at the background of the stingray picture near the beginning of this book. I created the "sand" by mixing ground black pepper with the clay. It made me sneeze!

Research is often an important part of the art that I create. I conduct my research in many ways. I go to libraries, zoos, museums and anyplace I can go to learn about the subject matter in my pictures. My favorite way to do research is going out in nature. Much of my research for this book was done by exploring an actual coral reef—what an adventure!

Marianne Berkes has spent much of her life with young children as a teacher, children's theater director and children's librarian. She knows how much children enjoy brilliantly illustrated counting books with predictable text about real animals. Recently retired to write full time and visit schools, she is the author of six picture books for children from Dawn

Publications, including her latest, *Going Home: The Mystery of Animal Migration*. Her website is: www.MarianneBerkes.com.

Jeanette Canyon received her Bachelor of Fine Arts degree from the Columbus College of Art & Design. Inspired by the philosophy and schools of Reggio Emilia, Italy, she enjoyed a distinguished career as an artist and arts educator of young children. She now spends her time creating art for children's books and visiting schools. She has illustrated two other books in

polymer clay, *Over in the Jungle* and *City Beats*. Jeanette's husband Christopher Canyon is also a renowned children's book artist.

Award-Winning Books by Marianne Berkes

Over in the Jungle by Marianne Berkes, a companion book to Over in the Ocean, features a tropical rainforest teeming with monkeys that hoot, ocelots that pounce, and boas that squeeze! Eye-popping illustrations by Jeanette Canyon are all in polymer clay.

Going Home: The Mystery of Animal Migration by Marianne Berkes, illustrated by Jennifer DiRubbio. By land, sea, and air, many animals migrate "home." Their remarkable journey is one of mystery and determination.

Over in the Arctic: Where the Cold Winds Blow by Marianne Berkes, illustrated by Jill Dubin. Children can learn about these amazing animals while they count, sing, and search for hidden animals.

Going Around the Sun: Some Planetary Fun by Marianne Berkes, illustrated by Janeen Mason. If Mother Sun were a poet, this is just what she would say to her beloved young family of planets!

Seashells by the Seashore by Marianne Berkes, illustrated by Robert Noreika. Children comb the beach, counting and identifying shells, and appreciating the creatures that lived in them.

Other Nature Books from Dawn Publications

The BLUES Go Birding Across America by Carol L. Malnor and Sandy F. Ferguson, illustrated by Lousie Schroeder. Five delightful cartoon bluebirds discover REAL birds—and what fun bird-watching can be.

This is the Sea that Feeds Us by Robert F. Baldwin, illustrated by Don Dyen. In simple cumulative verse, this book explores the oceans' fabulous food web that reaches all the way from plankton to people.

A Swim through the Sea is written and illustrated by Kristin Joy Pratt, the celebrated young "Eco-star" and author of vibrant books on subjects including the rain forest, the desert, wetlands, and flying creatures.

Eliza and the Dragonfly by Susie Caldwell Rinehart, illustrated by Anisa Claire Hovemann. Almost despite herself, Eliza becomes entranced by the "awful" dragonfly nymph, and soon both are transformed.

Dawn Publications is dedicated to inspiring in children a deeper understanding and appreciation for all life on Earth. To review our titles or to order, please visit us at www.dawnpub.com, or call 800-545-7475.